Skateboarding

by Marilyn Gould

**Published By
Capstone Press, Inc.
Mankato, Minnesota USA**

Distributed By
CHILDRENS PRESS®
CHICAGO

CIP
LIBRARY OF CONGRESS CATALOGING IN PUBLICATION DATA

Gould, Marilyn.
    Skateboarding / by Marilyn Gould.
        p. cm. – (Action sports)
    Summary: Describes the history, equipment, and techniques of skateboarding.

    ISBN 1-56065-048-6:
    1. Skateboarding – Juvenile literature. (1. Skateboarding) I. Title.
II. Title: Skateboarding. III. Series.
GV859.8.G67   1989
796.2'1 – dc20   89-27872
                                                CIP
                                                AC

PHOTO CREDITS
Photographs by Jamie Mosberg

Copyright ©1991 by Capstone Press, Inc. All rights reserved. No part of this book may be reproduced in any form without written permission from the publisher, except for brief passages included in a review. Printed in the United States of America.

CAPSTONE PRESS
Box 669, Mankato, MN 56001

Contents

Put Yourself on Wheels 5
Skateboards Start Rolling 6
On the Roll Again 16
Selecting your Skateboard 18
Safety on Wheels 26
Riding your Board 30
Tricks and Stunts 37
Thrashing 38
Happy Skateboarding 42
Glossary 45

Put Yourself on Wheels

How would you like to put yourself on wheels? Whether it is for going places, sport, or just plain fun, skateboarding is a great way to travel. A skateboard is light. It maneuvers better than a pair of roller skates. It needs no parking space and less repair than a bicycle. And, it is better exercise and more fun than a scooter.

Of course, it takes skill and know-how to ride a skateboard. You cannot just get on and take off. It will take time and practice to learn. It will take about the same amount of time as it takes to learn to ride a two-wheel bicycle. Then, once you have learned, you will probably want to spend a lot more time to get really good at it. You can try some tricks and work your way up to becoming a real **thrasher**.

You do not need a license to ride a skateboard. You do have to be careful, however, follow rules and think safety.

Many different kinds of skateboards are available at toy, sports, and special skateboard shops. At first, you may not be sure which kind of board to get. As you improve, you will know what is right for you. In time, you may become a **freestyler**. You may be so particular about the kind of board, **trucks**, and wheels you like, you will want to buy each separately and put them together for a real custom job. At the beginning buy a standard board that is not too expensive.

Speaking about beginning – let's see how skateboards and the sport of skateboarding got started.

Skateboards Start Rolling

Skateboarding became popular in the early 1960s. There were skateboards before that time, but they were pretty crude compared to the skateboards of today.

Your grandparents probably remember building their own skateboards. They would take apart a roller skate and nail a set of wheels to each end of a two-by-four piece of wood. If you saw someone riding one of those old-fashioned skateboards, you might laugh. Skateboarders then did not look like skateboarders of today. They stood very erect and straight on the board and did not bend their knees. They did not have the swaying motion of surfers riding a wave. Nor did they keep one foot in front of the other. They rode the boards like scooters, because that is what they were familiar with.

To move the board forward, they kept one foot on the board and one foot on the ground. When they gained a little speed they coasted with both feet parallel on the board. The trick was to keep their balance and not fall off if the hard metal wheels rode over a pebble or crack in the pavement. When they wanted to turn, they had to jump off the board, pick it up, and set it down in the right direction.

Some kids in those days would build the ultimate home-made vehicle. They called it an orange or apple crate scooter. They would nail an orange or apple crate on top of their skateboard. Then they would nail a broomstick across the top of the crate, to be used as a handle. Some enthusiastic builders went on to make go-carts. Some even competed in the All American Soap Box Derby that is still held every August in Akron, Ohio.

In the 1960s, however, things changed. Surfing became the new world-wide craze. Songs were written about surfing. Magazines and newspapers were filled with articles about surfers. Special cameras were invented to film surfers battling the waves. Boys copied the brushed-back hairstyles of the surfers. Some even dyed sun streaks in their hair. They switched from short

bathing trunks to cut-off jeans and pajama bottoms ripped off at the knees. Few girls surfed at that time.

It was during the surfing craze that a brainstorm came to a group of surfers at Val Surf, a surfboard shop in California. It dawned on them that skateboarding was not that different from surfing. Skateboarding was like sidewalk surfing. So with this brilliant idea in mind, they decided to start making skateboards. They felt it could become as popular as surfing. Before they could start producing skateboards, they needed to find a company that would supply them with the proper wheels and trucks. Trucks hold the **axle** of the wheels to the board and cushion the ride.

With a little research they found out that the Chicago Roller Skate Company made the best roller skates and had the best wheels. Val Surf wanted to buy just the wheels and trucks.

At first, the Chicago Roller Skate Company did not like the idea. They did not want their wheels separated from their shoes and mounted on a board. Finally, they gave in. Val surf was all set to start manufacturing skateboards.

They hired high school students to help them. Together they assembled, sanded, and finished the skateboards. As soon as the skateboards came off the line, there were customers. Val Surf had been right. Skate-boarding became as popular as surfing, and skateboards sold as fast as Val Surf could turn them out.

By 1965, skateboards were the biggest fad since yoyos. They were such a huge success that it looked as if they would never go out of style. Kids all over the world were riding skateboards and loving every minute of it. But some people were not so pleased. They started knocking skateboards, saying they were a nuisance.

They said skateboards made too much noise, and they did. The harder wheels used at that time were very noisy, They said it was not safe to walk. Skateboarders were everywhere. Wherever there was a stretch of concrete someone would whiz by on a skateboard. They were in parks, neighborhoods and on busy city streets.

Drivers worried about hitting skateboarders. Some skateboarders did not look where they were going. They rode their skateboards across the street. They darted out between cars into traffic.

The final straw came when doctors said there were too many skateboard injuries. Kids were getting broken arms, broken legs, sprained an-

kles, and head and back injuries. It was reported that skateboards were more dangerous than bicycles and the major cause of childhood injuries.

Word spread that skateboards were unsafe and should be taken off the market. Cities started passing laws to ban skateboarding on public streets. Some cities tried to outlaw skateboards altogether. Parents stopped allowing their children to ride them. In no time there were hardly any skateboards around. It looked like the end for skateboarding.

It was surprising that something as popular as skateboarding could suddenly disappear. Most kids gave up their skateboards. No one seemed to be riding them or buying them. Makers of skateboards and owners of skateboard shops went out of business. Skateboard competitions were cancelled.

Only a few skateboarders loved their skateboards so much that they refused to give them up. They saw skateboarding as an art, and they wanted to become great skateboard athletes. These skateboarders practiced many hours each day. At first they chose safe places away from traffic, where they would not disturb anyone.

The more these skateboarders practiced, the better they became at doing tricks. Soon they began trying new and more daring tricks, and that's when they found out that the equipment was not good enough. The skateboards needed to be quieter, less dangerous, and better made.

The skateboarders wanted to experiment with the skateboards to see how to improve them and how much they could do with them before they would break. But to do that they needed a place where they did not have to worry about making noise or being too cautious about trying anything risky.

They decided they had to break the rules and go "underground." Skateboarders began to try out difficult tricks secretly in deserted places. They skated in pipelines, sewers, and empty swimming pools. There are no statistics on how many got hurt. But, like test pilots, they tried all sorts of things. They became experts on the problems of skateboards and skateboarding.

The trucks and wheels, originally designed for roller skates, were not right for skateboards. The trucks did not have enough cushion or give. The wheels were made of a hard clay which made them noisy and too smooth to grip the ground.

Anything beyond a slow turn was difficult to control. That is why so many people were "sliding-out" and hurting themselves.

Little by little the few skateboarders who kept on testing skateboards learned what to do to make the boards easier to control and safer. They worked out new maneuvers and stunts. They helped make skateboarding what it is today.

On The Roll Again

In the ten years that most people thought skateboarding had disappeared, many exciting things were happening in the world of technology.

Urethane, a soft durable plastic, was invented. Makers of roller skates thought it would be a good material for skate wheels. It made the wheels slower and quieter. They gripped better. But they did not sell because roller skaters were not interested in going slower. And they did not care about noise.

In 1973 a surfer, named Frank Nasworthy, heard about urethane. He thought it would be a perfect material for skateboard wheels. He went to the president of a company who made urethane roller skate wheels that were not selling. After some discussion, they decided to go into business together. They started making Cadillac Wheels, the first urethane wheels made for skateboards.

Then Nasworthy met with his friend Bob Bahne, who made surfboards. He showed him the new urethane wheels for skateboards and asked him if he could make a better board for skateboards.

Bahne found out that laminated fiberglass had just the right flexibility. When the rider pushed down and raised up to make turns and control speed, the fiberglass board would give and snap back and stay with the rider. Yet it was durable enough not to crack or wear out.

Nasworthy had increased the performance of the trucks and wheels. Bahne had come up with a better blank (board). The result? A new and improved, safer, quieter, super skateboard.

The major problems that had brought skateboarding to a halt were solved. Enough time had gone by for people to forget their outrage and nervousness about skateboards. Besides, many parents had an entirely different attitude about skateboarding. They had skateboarded, themselves, in the 1960s. They had fond memories of skateboarding and wanted their children to have the same fun. They did not think of it as a fad. They considered it an action sport that was fun and good exercise. It took precision and grace to do well.

Skateboards were on the roll again. It seemed that, overnight, skateboard shops opened up. Skateboard parks and bowls, safe and supervised, were built. Hotdoggers could practice their daredevil stunts and go vertical defying gravity around the sides of a concrete bowl. Special clothing and protective equipment such as helmets, knee and elbow pads, and padded sweaters were designed. These could ward off bruises and **road rashes**.

Skateboarding was back for good.

Selecting Your Skateboard

Certain things about skateboards are always the same – they all have a board, trucks, and wheels. Skateboards, like other sports equipment, have different models to suit different riders, according to where and how they are going to ride. In selecting a skateboard, you need to consider your size, how long you have been riding, how good you are, and for what purpose you will be using your board.

For instance, the length of the board depends

on your height and weight. You should choose the shape by how comfortably your feet fit on the board. A beginner will have an easier time with a board that is only slightly flexible. A thrasher (or expert) will want a board with a lot more give. If handstands or downhill racing is something you want to try, a rigid board is for you.

Before you choose a board, decide whether you will use it for transportation, competition, street skating, or riding ramps. Or maybe you just want to hang out and have a little fun and exercise.

Spend a little time thinking about these things before you buy a board. In the long run it will cut down your shopping time, and you will have a better chance of getting the right board.

The Board

Boards (also called blanks or decks) come in different lengths. If you are a beginning skateboarder you will probably want a basic board (29 inches), which is the best length for street use. Shorter boards (27 inches) are good for stunts and **freestyle**. Longer boards (30 inches) are used for verticals (riding ramps) and downhill (speed racing).

For the proper length, you should consider your height and weight. The taller and heavier you are, the longer the board you need.

The shape can be a matter of taste, but it is also a good idea to see how comfortably your feet fit on the board. A hammerhead or notched nose may be good for skating ramps and for grabbing your board. A **kicktail** – an end that curves up – will be necessary for certain tricks.

Boards are made of wood, fiberglass, and aluminum. At one time plastic was used and considered the best. Now almost all boards are made of seven-ply maple. Plywood is considered the standard material for pro boards.

A board with a little **flex** is probably good for the beginning and average skateboarder. The flex gives a softer, smoother ride over rough terrain. It helps in making sharp turns. It makes it easier to **weight** and **unweight** (keeping both feet on the board, pushing down and rising up to control speed).

A board with a lot of flex or give can be difficult to use. It is hard to keep your balance. Everytime you move you will feel the board sag under you, then bounce back. In time, when you can handle that kind of **snap** or **punch** it may be exactly what you like in a board.

The surface of the board is another choice. Some boards are smooth. Others have a bumpy deck to keep your feet from slipping. If the surface of your board is smooth, use grip tape,

even if it means covering the design. It is more important to stay on the board than to show it off.

Trucks

Trucks are metal units that attach to the board. They hold the axle for the wheels and cushions. The cushions act as shock absorbers.

In the 1970s many pre-assembled skateboards were not particularly good. The best ones were very expensive. So skateboarders would buy each part separately. Then they would put them together to make their own custom skateboards.

When buying parts, skateboarders pay a lot of attention to the trucks. They should be lightweight, yet made of a sturdy material that will be safe and strong. The cushions in the trucks have to be extra spongy. This allows the board to ride smoothly over rough spots without shocking the rider's legs.

Skateboarders of the 70s were particular. They discussed the hanger plate and the bushing and the nuts and the bolts and on and on. That was all they talked about. Anyone who was not into skateboards could not understand a word they were saying.

Today's skaters who enter competitions still assemble their own skateboards. They are particular about the trucks they select. Many buy skateboards already assembled. Because skateboards have to pass certain safety standards, the trucks have to be safe and made properly.

Wheels

Urethane wheels have taken almost all the noise and jerkiness out of skateboarding. The old clay wheels picked up tiny pieces of gravel, jammed the skateboard into a skid, and broke.

Urethane wheels last much longer and do not break easily. A pebble will not jam them and a bump on the sidewalk will not stop them. They even ride smoothly on dirt and grass. The only problem with urethane is that it is slippery on a wet surface.

Wheels come in different widths, diameters, and degrees of softness. A softer wheel gives a smoother ride and a harder wheel goes faster. Soft wheels are good for beginning street skating, medium for regular street, and hard for skating ramps. The larger the wheel, the better the balance. They are easier to learn on than smaller wheels. Experienced skaters prefer smaller wheels which are lighter and faster.

The bearings of most wheels are sealed and encased to keep them clean, grit-free, and quiet. People are no longer disturbed by noisy skateboards. A quieter ride makes it easier for the skateboarder to listen for any oncoming cars.

Tools For Your Skateboard

It is a good idea to have a few tools to fix or adjust your skateboard. If you cannot find a skateboard parts store, go to a hardware store. Take your board along and ask the salesperson for a wrench and screwdriver that will be the right size for your board.

If you are a beginner, it might be best to start with a standard board that is not too expensive. You will want to spend a lot of time practicing to get really good at skateboarding. Then, like some thrashers, you might end up with a quiver of skateboards, each for a different purpose.

Safety on Wheels

Even though skateboarding has become a lot safer than it used to be, it is still a moving sport. In any sport, particularly a moving sport, you can fall. Falls cause scrapes, sprains, bruises and broken bones. At one time skateboarders bragged about their road rashes, raspberries,

burgers, and **dings**. It is much smarter to try to prevent injuries.

Olympic champions are a perfect example of super athletes who do incredibly difficult things. They push themselves to the limit, but take every precaution to keep their bodies intact. They know that if they get hurt they cannot compete, so they are very careful to avoid accidents.

Olympic athletes make sure their equipment is in perfect condition. Before you get on your skateboard, you should check to see that your trucks are securely fastened to the blank and that all the screws and nuts are properly tightened. See that the wheels spin properly.

You should also make sure that you, the skater, are in tip-top condition, so your body works well. Like any well-trained athlete, you should eat good nutritious food and be well-rested. Develop your muscles by exercising everyday, and warm up with some bends and twists before you start your ride.

You may have noticed that athletes on television wear the correct clothing. When you ride your skateboard, particularly if you are a beginner, you should wear high-top sneakers that will grip the board. Wear long pants, a long sleeved shirt rolled around the elbow, gloves, elbow and knee pads, and a helmet.

There are certain unsafe places you should never ride your skateboard. If you see a sign that says "No skateboards," get off your board and walk. You should never ride in the middle of the street or in heavy traffic. Riding in sewers, pipelines or empty swimming pools is dangerous.

Never skate on wet or damp pavement. Urethane wheels slip when they are wet, and you can be seriously hurt. Besides, water is not good for the bearings. If it begins to rain, keep your board dry under your arm. Even on dry days it is a good idea to watch out for wet spots.

Accidents can happen if you try something too soon. Freestylers can make skateboarding look easy, but it takes a long time to learn how to ride a skateboard with ease and grace. You have to practice and be patient. It is foolish to do a stunt or a trick because someone else can do it. When you are ready, try it slowly and carefully. Do not go down a steep hill or try to go as fast as you can.

Last, but not least, learn how to fall. A relaxed fall can keep you from getting hurt while skateboarding. Professional athletes who play soccer, football and almost every sport take terrible falls and get back up hardly fazed. They've practiced how to fall gracefully.

These are some of the things you should practice on a soft surface, like the grass or a mat:

- Bend your knees and lower your body as you go into a fall.
- Roll yourself into a ball (protecting your head, arms, elbows, and hands).
- Continue to roll several times after the fall.
- Relax and be flexible.
- Keep from reaching out and stopping your fall with your hands.

Riding Your Board

Getting To Know Your Board

Learning to ride a skateboard takes time and practice. It is very much like learning to ride a bicycle. You need balance and nerve while you are in motion, and it will take patience and, perhaps, a few falls before you have mastered it.

It is very hard to stand on a board when it is not moving. If you want to see how your board feels before you learn to ride it, put it on a flat surface and hold onto someone or something. With support you can see how your feet fit on it, how it wobbles from side to side, and how it tips in front and back. When you are first learning, you may want to adjust your board so it is not too wobbly.

Flat tracking

Flat tracking is the first thing to try. Take your board to a flat, smooth, safe place like a park, playground, or backyard. Put one foot straight on the board behind the front wheels. Leave room for your back foot to go behind your front foot, but do not stand so far forward that the board tips.

Give a little push with your other foot as if you were riding a scooter. Do not try to put both feet on yet. Just pedal around to get a feel of your board in motion. This is called flat tracking or **pedaling**.

See which foot feels more comfortable on the front of the board. If it is your left foot, you are "**standard**" or "**regular**" **footed**. If it is your right foot, you are a "**goofy foot**." It does not matter which way you ride. Skateboarders do what is comfortable for them, and either way is right.

Riding down a slight incline

When you feel ready, take your board to a place that has a very slight incline and is safe from cars or pedestrians. Perhaps there is a little slope in the same playground, park, or backyard where you have been practicing your flat tracking. Driveways are not very safe because you can easily roll into the street.

Your board should be facing down the incline. Put your first foot straight on the board behind the front wheels and give a little push with your other foot just as you have already practiced. Now put your pushing foot behind your front foot and across, or perpendicular to, the board. At the same time, turn your front foot so it is across the board too.

Keep your knees slightly bent and lean a little toward the front or nose of the board. When you do this "you are going for it." It is natural to want to lean back, away from the hill but, just as in skiing and surfing, it is wrong and will make you lose your balance.

Keep your arms loose and away from your body. If you feel you are going to fall or if you want to get off, step off the front or side of the board. The board may scoot behind you, but you will be firmly on the ground.

Keep trying this until you feel relaxed and comfortable.

Turning

When you feel you have control, you can try a turn. To learn to make turns, you must think of your body as two halves; the top half above your waist and the bottom half below your waist.

Your top half always faces down the incline or the "fall line" of the hill. Your shoulders stay level, your arms are loose, and your head and eyes look straight ahead. Your bottom half is the part that maneuvers and turns the board.

To turn in the direction your toes are pointing (a front side turn), put your weight on the side of the board your toes are on. Remember, your feet are across the board. The board will tilt down a little under your toes and turn in that direction. More weight makes a sharper turn. Less weight makes a more gradual turn. Try it over and over until you have got the hang of it.

Now try a turn in the direction of your heels (a backside turn). Put weight on the side of the board your heels are on. The board will tilt slightly under your heels and turn that way.

Always keep your top half facing forward, your knees slightly bent, and your arms loose. In time you will not have to think so much about what you are doing. You will quite naturally shift your weight and lean in the direction you want to turn.

Try riding your board slowly on a straight line; then try a curved line. Practice until you have it just right. You will know you are getting there when you can "weight and unweight" easily.

When you have mastered that, you can try a slow **slalom** course. Set up objects or markers in a line with spaces in between. Try weaving or wedeling (pronounced vay-delling) around them.

Take one step at a time and be patient and persistent. All of a sudden it will happen. You will be moving, with a swing and a sway, feeling as if the board were an extension of your body.

Tricks and Stunts

All sorts of tricks can be done on skateboards, but they should be tried only by skillful riders who have perfect control. Wear protective clothing–helmet, gloves, high-top sneakers, and pads for knees, elbows, and wrists.

There are three basic kinds of tricks: **street**, freestyle, and **vertical**.

Street skating can be done almost anywhere, but some street tricks are extremely difficult. You should not try them until you are really good at keeping your balance when you crouch or bend low on the board. Some of the tricks done on the street are: kick-turns, **tic-tacs**, berts, grinds, **ollies**, and slides.

Freestyle is usually done in competitions. The challenge is to do a variation of difficult, stylish tricks in one or two minutes, without falling. Some of the freestylers favorites are: **wheelie**s, **50/50s**, caspers, handstands, and popos.

Vertical tricks are done on ramps and put the skater into the air. They are very difficult, very dangerous, and should be tried only by advanced skaters wearing proper protective gear. Some of the tricks tried by airborne skaters are: carves, **airs**, inverts, fakies, and eggplants.

Thrashing

Now that skateboarding is back it has a new image. Skateboarders call themselves "thrashers." They twist, spin and rotate their bodies in fancy maneuvers, pushing themselves to new limits. They work long hard hours creating new tricks and stunts. With concentration and practice they train their bodies to perform.

Why? Because skateboarding is no longer just a fad or a form of transportation. It is a competitive sport. There are amateur and professional

39

competitions at which skaters compete and spectators come to watch with amazement.

The National Skateboard Association runs professional tours and amateur competitions. They have organized amateur contests into three regions, each having two districts:

Eastern Region (southern and northeastern states)

Central Region (southern and northcentral states)

Western Region (southern and northwestern states)

To compete in the national championships, usually held in late December, an amateur must first qualify at a district contest which is limited to forty skaters. Fifteen of these forty will qualify to go on to a regional competition. Of the thirty skaters who compete in each region, ten finalists and two alternates advance to the national championships.

There are three judges in amateur competitions (five for professional), and there are three types of events:

Freestyle is a run of tricks like handstands, flips, wheelies, space walks, and assorted spins that are often done to music. This event is judged not only by the variety and difficulty of tricks but by the grace and style of the performer and how the routine goes with the music.

Streetstyle is skating on and over obstacles, jumping ramps, and riding walls. Judges look for difficulty, variety, and the number of tricks executed successfully.

Vertical ramp, the most spectacular, is a display of aerial tricks. Judges give points for originality and difficulty, the way in which the skater uses the entire skating area, and how the skater performs to the limit without losing control. Though a skater may be penalized for falling, the judges consider how the fall affected the rest of the run and the difficulty of the attempted trick.

Skateboarding or "thrashing," either for competition or for fun, has become an accepted sport. There are an estimated 1.5 million skateboarders nationwide and another one million around the world.

Happy Skateboarding

One of the reasons skateboarding is here to stay is that it has become an established sport. Skateboarders all over the world practice at a high risk-taking level in order to enter competitions. Someday skateboarding may even become an event included in the Olympics. Stunts now being done certainly take extreme athletic training and physical ability.

Another reason that skateboarding never really died is that it is a wonderful means of transportation. It makes getting there fun – with no fumes. Many kids ride to school on their skateboards. Some adults prefer a skateboard to a bus or car when they go to work. A number of travelers have found that a skateboard fits easily in their backpacks. They would not leave home without them.

Mail and newspapers are delivered on skateboards in some towns. Even policemen have been seen doing their rounds on a board. Some people interested in exercising every day would rather ride a board than jog, and they do long distance and marathon runs.

Let's face it, skateboarding is not only fun and good exercise, but it is a way to move. It is body language, a creative form of expression. So get **stoked**, thrashers, and start ripping.

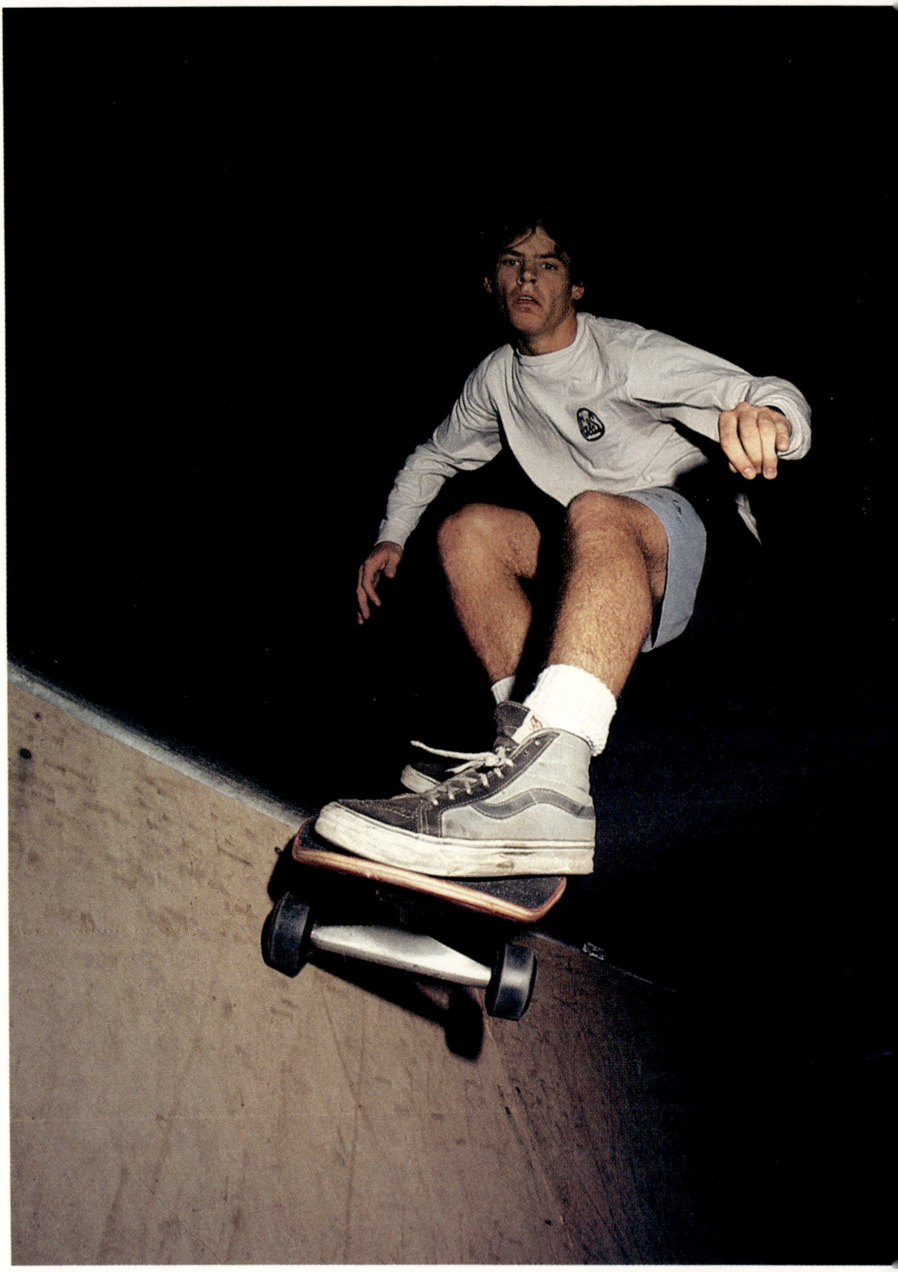

Glossary

Air: A trick putting the skater in the air while grabbing the board.

Axles: The bar or rod on which a wheel turns.

Dings: A bruise.

50/50: A slide on both axles or trucks done in vertical skating.

Flat tracking or pedaling: Pushing and gliding on a flat surface.

Flex: The bending or give of a board.

Freestyle: Graceful riding and tricks done in competition.

Freestylers: Skateboarders who do tricks.

Goofy foot: Riding with the right foot forward.

Kicktail: The angled (curved) tail of a board necessary for some tricks.

Ollie: Flying forward through the air without grabbing the board.

Road rashes, raspberries, and burgers: Dings or bruises.

Slalom: Riding around markers or cones.

Snap or punch: The way a board comes back after it has flexed.

Standard or regular foot: Riding with the left foot forward.

Stoked: Ready for action, excited.

Street: The style of skating on sidewalks, curbs, and street-type ramps.

Thrasher: Skateboarding expert.

Tic-tac: Kick turning left and right in rapid succession.

Truck: The unit that holds the wheels, axles, and bearings.

Vertical: Skating on ramps and, usually, doing air tricks.

Wheelie: Balancing on one set of wheels with the other end up.

Weighting and unweighting: Standing and squatting on the board.

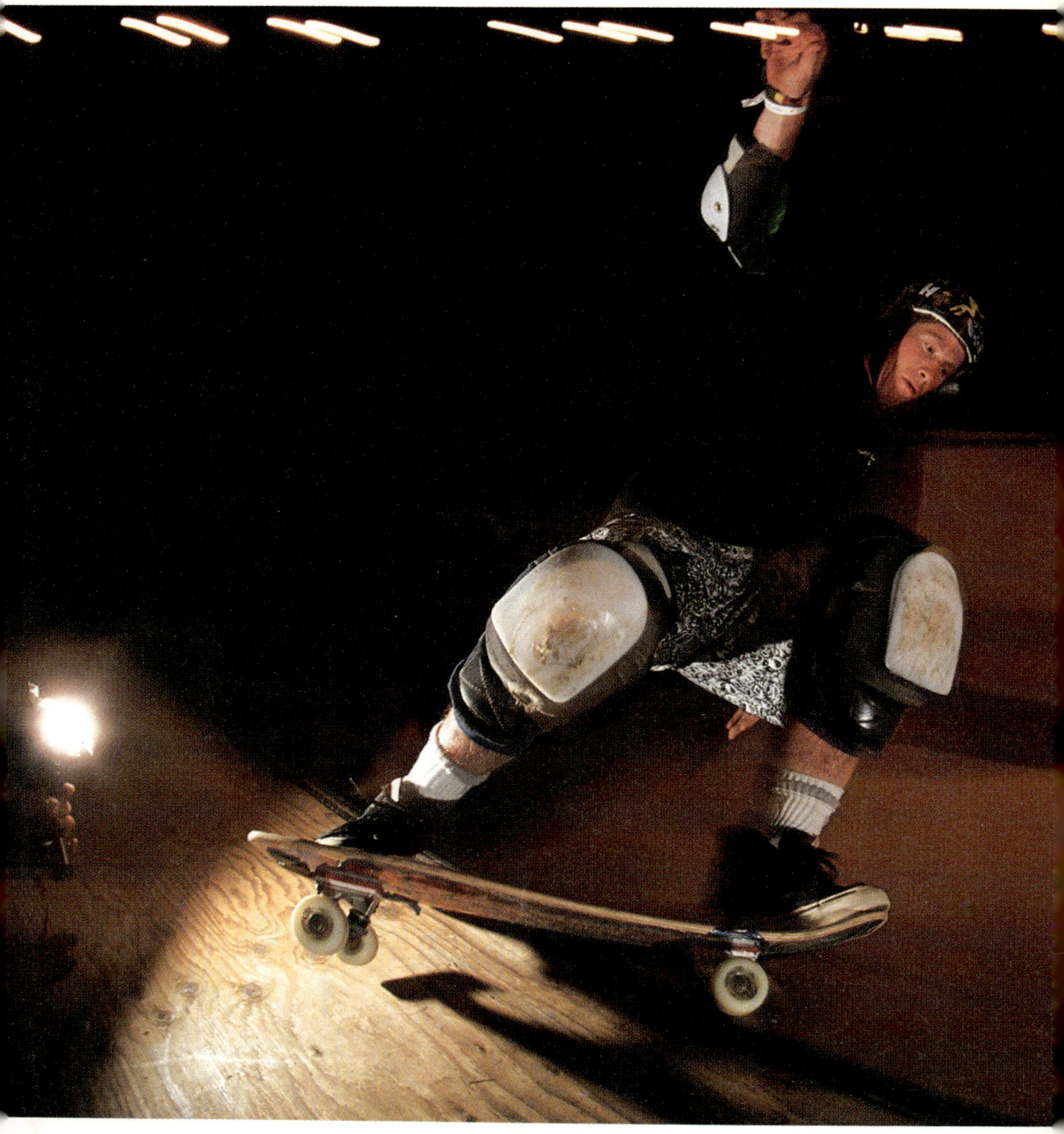

48